# Zen Pig and Friends
# Holiday
## Coloring Book

created by:
# mark brown

Dedicated to all the parents, grandparents, teachers, and caregivers that are being brave for the children in their lives during this transitional time.

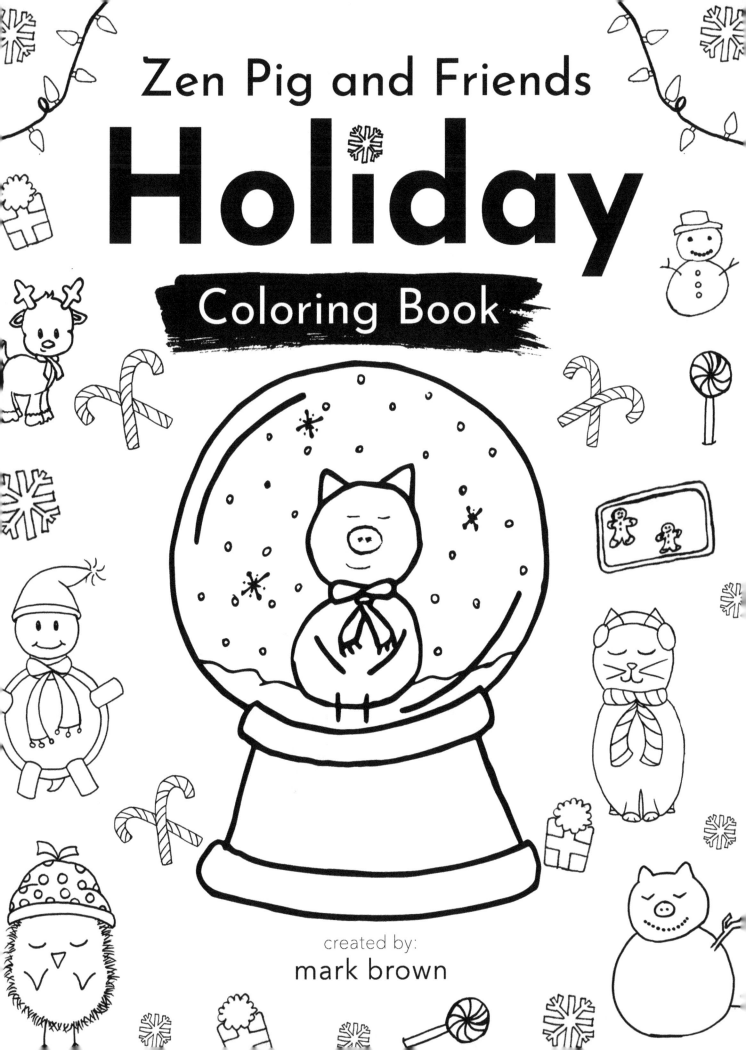

# Hello Friends!

In the following pages, you will find yourself with some really fun coloring and activity pages. These activities will help you with focus and with the ability to unwind, even if just a bit, which will allow you to have a wonderful day.

The only rule is to have fun. So pick your favorite colors and get ready to have an amazing time.

Let Zen Pig and Friends make your days happy and jolly with their holiday festivities!

# EACH DAY IS A GIFT!

# How to Draw Zen Pig!

1.

2.

3.

4.

5.

6.

7.

Let's See Your Zen Pig!

# Draw Your Zen Pig!

# Help Zen Pig & Friends choose a hat!

## Draw a line to help them choose

# Can you help Zen Pig decorate snowmen?

Can you help Zen Pig
decorate candy canes?

# Can you help Zen Pig color in his new friend?

# Help Zen Pig finish making his gingerbread man.

Draw your favorite
holiday treat above!

candy

cane

# Tic-Tac-Mistletoe!

# Color me!

Color me!

# Color me!

# THANKFUL!

# 365

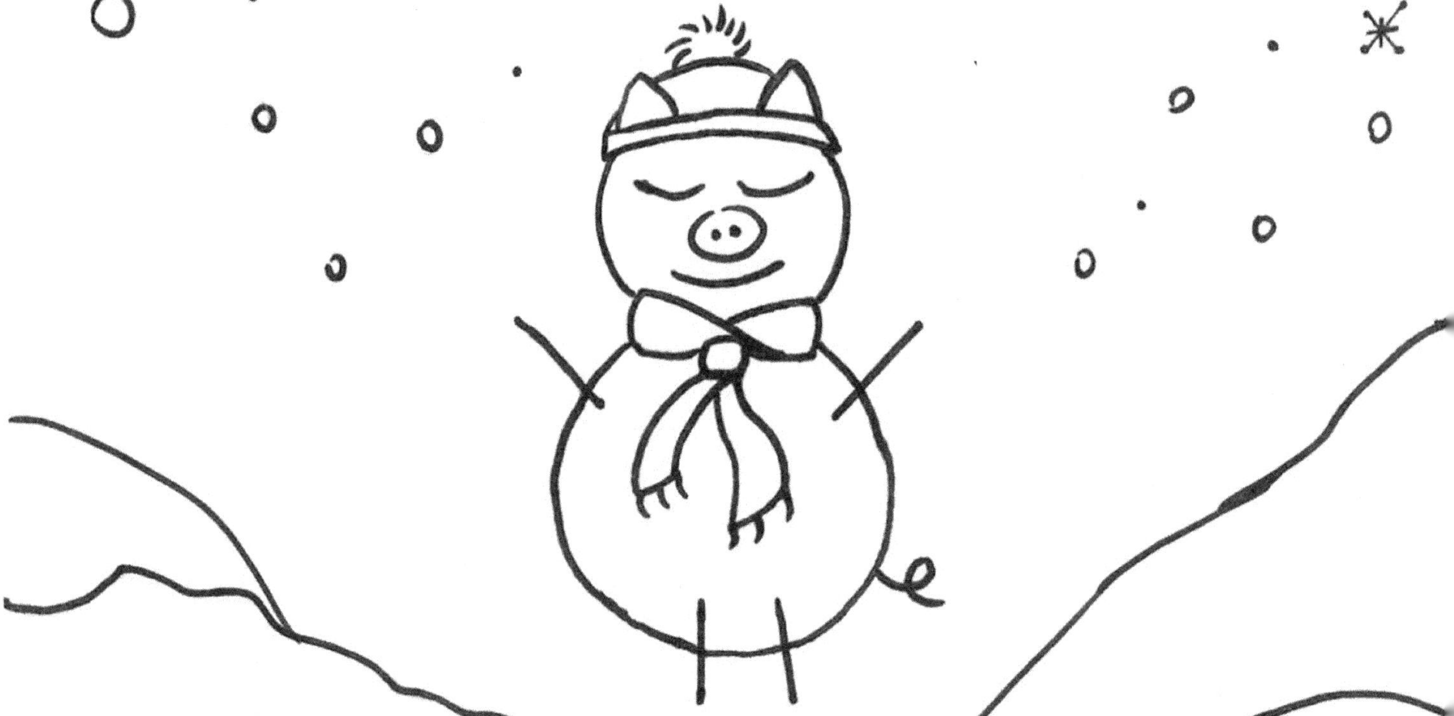

```
G  S  C  J  A  J  R  P  W  C  D  G  N  Q  M
N  S  E  O  P  Q  T  E  X  K  F  L  O  V  E
K  E  T  L  M  G  B  D  S  N  O  W  M  A  N
C  N  S  M  O  P  R  Y  D  F  N  M  H  B  V
I  L  A  U  W  P  A  A  Z  M  Y  O  C  Z  T
H  U  M  C  A  C  A  S  T  K  L  W  I  I  W
C  F  A  E  A  F  E  L  S  I  Q  L  D  V  Z
J  D  N  T  X  O  W  L  D  I  T  J  L  M  Y
B  N  B  L  G  D  D  A  T  Q  O  U  N  O  U
T  I  D  Q  P  A  Y  I  A  R  F  N  D  P  B
P  M  E  C  E  S  P  C  A  K  U  S  O  E  H
K  S  D  N  E  I  R  F  N  W  P  T  W  S  V
H  N  V  C  X  S  O  A  X  F  U  J  H  K  E
K  U  E  V  S  R  H  J  D  T  Q  K  C  G  A
X  D  K  Z  G  T  Y  D  N  F  R  B  X  Y  Z
```

| Love | Chick |
|------|-------|
| Friends | Snowman |
| Gratitude | Namaste |
| Turtle | Holidays |
| Zen | Cat |
| Compassion | Thankful |

Make lasting memories with
Zen Pig and his friends this holiday season!

Namaste to all,
and to all a good night!

CPSIA information can be obtained
at www.ICGtesting.com
Printed in the USA
LVHW012348021121
702316LV00007B/98